T0368260

Livingston's Tales

The Beginning

Carollynn Lopez

AuthorHouse™
1663 Liberty Drive
Bloomington, IN 47403
www.authorhouse.com
Phone: 1 (800) 839-8640

Published by AuthorHouse   01/11/2019

ISBN: 978-1-5462-7499-5 (sc)
ISBN: 978-1-5462-7500-8 (e)

Library of Congress Control Number: 2019900238

Print information available on the last page.

Any people depicted in stock imagery provided by Getty Images are models,
and such images are being used for illustrative purposes only.
Certain stock imagery © Getty Images.

This book is printed on acid-free paper.

Because of the dynamic nature of the Internet, any web addresses or links contained
in this book may have changed since publication and may no longer be valid. The views
expressed in this work are solely those of the author and do not necessarily reflect the
views of the publisher, and the publisher hereby disclaims any responsibility for them.

authorHOUSE®

TABLE OF CONTENTS

AUTHOR'S NOTE

Some of the words used in this book you may not understand. Don't worry! At the end of the book is a glossary with the definitions of some of the more difficult words. While reading, you will see words marked with an asterisk (*). These are words that can be found in the glossary with the definition.

Words are an essential part of our everyday lives. Having a vast vocabulary can open so many doors for you! Doors into far away worlds, into our past, into our future, and into our dreams! Never stop expanding your vocabulary and your mind!!

Your friend,
Carollynn Lopez

This book is dedicated to my children; Kel, Keenan, and Markie. You are my endless inspiration and my greatest gifts!!

PROLOGUE

The attic was dark and smelled of dust and time. At the top of the pull-down steps stood an older woman. She pushed one of her red curls from in front of her kind blue eyes and scanned the room. She climbed the rest of the way into the attic and fumbled for the pull-chain. There… found it! One quick yank and the light turned the shadowy shapes into clear images of boxes and old furniture. She walked around clearing the cobwebs that stood guard over the aged treasures. A smile warmed her face as she spotted her old hope chest in the corner. The layer of dust that had accumulated* on it over the years reminded her of powdered sugar on a brownie. She grabbed a piece of cloth from a nearby basket, wiped the dust from the chest and opened the latch with a sharp *click*. She slowly lifted the lid which made a low creaking moan in protest* to being disturbed after such a long slumber. Moving aside her prom dress, a keepsake from her adolescence*, she found what she had been seeking. He was a bit worn but instantly lit up her face with love and nostalgia*. Livingston was a sandy brown stuffed bunny with long fuzzy ears and a small tan nose. The whiskers on one side of his little round face were missing from years of play. She gathered him up and smiled at him. "I have a very special surprise for you today, my old friend!"

CHAPTER ONE
THE MOVE

Kel was eight years old. He was a very bright and very small boy for his age. He had just moved from Orlando, Florida with his mother and little brother to this new home in Illinois. Orlando was a big city with tons of people, buses that would take you nearly anywhere you wanted to go at nearly any time, and lights everywhere. They had lived in an apartment complex with a pool, a big pond, a clubhouse and a playground. He couldn't remember ever having seen snow or icicles. On Christmas Day they would open their gifts then go swimming and have a BBQ.

Momma said it would be much different here. It certainly was! Instead of a big city with a lot of traffic and stores everywhere that were open all day and night, they now lived in a small village. It was called The Village of Oakwood Hills and there wasn't a single store or restaurant and very few street lights! There was, however, a beach across the street from their new house that had a small playground with swings, a slide, a merry-go-round and a jungle gym.

The house they moved into was a big change too. There were no neighbors living upstairs or right next door and there were only four houses on the whole block, including theirs. Momma said that the Village had been named for the lot on which they now lived. It was the longest and steepest* hill with the oldest Oak tree in the whole village. The big thick tree stood at the top of the property, its trunk tall and strong, yet many of the branches bent over and nearly covered a small garden shed which was placed at the far edge of the front lawn. Kel couldn't help thinking that it looked as though it were leaning on the small shed, much like one of his elderly neighbors from the apartments in Orlando had leaned on the railings surrounding the pool area when they would get winded.

He instantly loved this new house. There was a small flat area that made the front yard, another right out the back door and a steep hill that bordered it all like a picture frame. A small stand of trees on the far west side of the yard hid the home from people traveling down Lakeview Drive. As soon as Kel saw the yard he imagined all the things he could do! He could roll down the long hill until he was too dizzy to stand and he couldn't wait for it to snow so he could go sledding!

One of his favorite things to do was to play with his Playmobil™ Cowboys and Indians outside and make wonderful cities for them. For the Indians, he used the garden hose to make long rivers flowing down a smaller dirt hill that led from the front yard to the side yard. There were hunting grounds in the old overgrown garden and a tee-pee village between the two. For the Cowboys he made big forts by the old stone pit not far from the bottom of the little river and small towns tracing the shallow steps that led down along the east side of the house to the backyard. He imagined wonderful games to play and wars to fight and adventures to have. Still, he felt that all these things would be so much more fun if he had even one friend to join him in his games.

Being new to this place he didn't really know anyone yet. Well, there was always Keenan, his little brother, but he was only four years old and couldn't play any decent games or go on adventures or anything that was any real fun. All the things he could do with his little brother were pretty boring. Keenan couldn't even play any good board games! Only ones like Candyland and Chutes and Ladders. Kel was much too old to play baby games like that!

CHAPTER TWO
THE GIFT

One day Kel's Grammy and Papa came to visit. Kel was so excited because, having lived so far away before, he didn't get to see them much. Now they lived just outside the Village, only a short six blocks from him! His mother said that once he knew the area better he could walk to their house all by himself. He was looking forward to that! Kel loved them dearly and visiting with them was one of his favorite things in the whole wide world!

When they got there Grammy announced that she had gifts for her grandsons! Kel got very excited! Grammy and Papa always gave the best gifts! Grammy was the one who had given him his Cowboys and Indians and Papa had sent him a telescope last Christmas so he could look at the moon and stars. He couldn't wait to see what they had brought for him this time! He would have to wonder what was in the package for a little bit longer, though. Since Keenan was younger he got to open his first.

After Keenan made slow tedious* work of ripping the paper off his gift, one little piece at a time, he found a big foamy puzzle made up of only 6 pieces which were each about the size of a place mat for the dinner table. Kel wondered why in the world anyone would want to do a puzzle like that. How hard could it possibly be anyway? But Keenan loved it!

For Kel, Grammy had a package shaped like a shoe box and wrapped in bright yellow paper. Finally Grammy nodded to him, letting him know it was his turn! He tore into the wrapping and threw the lid off the box! Inside there was a lump beneath orange tissue paper. As his excitement grew, Kel grabbed the tissue paper, flung it aside and discovered a stuffed bunny. Kel blinked and then tried very hard not to let his disappointment* show. *A stuffed bunny*, he thought... *why would Grammy give me a baby toy like a stuffed bunny?* He quickly smiled up at Grammy with the best smile he could manage and said, "Thank you, Grammy... I, um... he's cute."

Grammy could tell that it wasn't what Kel had expected but she was a bit tickled by how gracious* he was trying to be. She leaned over and whispered into Kel's ear, "This isn't just any ordinary stuffed animal" as she gave him an ominous* wink. Kel looked at her with confusion*. Grammy looked around and saw that Momma was busy with Keenan, who was now trying desperately to piece together his new puzzle, and noticed that Papa had lost himself in a program on TV, so she took Kel into the next room.

"Kel," She said in a formal tone, "I would like you to meet Livingston!" She gestured* to the bunny still in the box, lying in a nest of the remaining tissue paper. "Livingston", she announced waving towards the skeptical* little boy, "this is my grandson, Kel." She smiled and then said, "Kel's in a new town and needs a friend. I know that I haven't been able to spend the time with you that I had when I was a child." She spoke to the stuffed animal, with a bit of sadness in her voice, as if she had to give away a family pet or let go of an old friend.

Kel looked closely at his Grammy with sincere concern. "Grammy… are you OK?" He asked carefully. "It's just a stuffy… I don't think it cares."

Grammy gasped and put her hands over Livingston's long fuzzy ears. "Kel… I told you…. This isn't just *any* stuffed animal!" she said barely louder than a whisper. Then she picked Livingston up out of the box and set him gingerly* upon her lap. "Livingston is very special!" she explained with a proud smile. "My mother bought him for me a long time ago when I was not much older than you are now. It wasn't too long after that that she became ill. I was so sad and scared while she was sick. My mother and I were very close, you know. A lot like you and your mother. I used to snuggle up tight with Livingston at night and when my mother passed away I laid on my bed, squeezing him, and cried."

Kel listened to Grammy's story feeling very sad. He had never met his Great-Grandmother but he couldn't imagine losing his Momma. The thought made his eyes well up with tears. He listened as Grammy continued, trying to quickly blink them away.

"My tears fell onto Livingston's fuzzy ears. And then the most amazing thing happened!" Grammy's voice got very quiet and very mysterious.

CHAPTER THREE

LIVINGSTON

Kel was more than a little curious as to what this amazing thing was. Grammy looked around carefully, then leaned even closer to Kel and whispered very slowly, "Livingston's ear … twitched!"

Kel gasped and looked at Livingston in wonder! "By itself?" he asked.

"Yes!" Grammy said excitedly, "All by itself! Then he wrapped his little paws around my neck and *hugged me back!*"

Kel was filled with excitement and wonder! Then he started to consider* what had just been said. He looked at Grammy with his eyes squinted and half smiling, "You're just telling me fairy tales, Grammy!" he giggled.

"No! Honestly, sweetheart! Livingston is *alive*... as alive as you and I!" She looked around carefully again as she warned him, "but don't *ever* tell <u>anyone</u>! If people knew they would take him away from you and run all sorts of tests on him... and on you too, I shouldn't wonder!" She paused thoughtfully then said with a suspicious* voice, "If he would even come to life for anyone else."

They both looked slowly over at Livingston in anticipation*. Livingston just sat there on Grammy's lap, unmoving. Just when Kel began losing hope... Livingston *winked*! Kel jumped up with a start and yelled in excitement, "Did you see? Did you see!!?" He started jumping and dancing around.

Kel's Mom ran into the room. "What's all the yelling about? Is everything alright?"

Grammy quickly spoke up, "Oh, yes... everything's just fine!" She shot Kel a quick glance and he sat down and giggled nervously*. "We're just playing with Livingston, that's all!" She said with a cheery voice and a wide grin then stood up saying, "Go on, now and let us alone! We're having fun!" as she shooed* Momma out of the room.

Momma smiled and with a little laugh headed downstairs to the kitchen to start supper. Before Grammy could say anything Kel quickly apologized, "I'm sorry Grammy! I was just so excited! I'll keep it a secret! I promise!!"

Grammy just laughed and kissed Kel on the forehead. "I know you will. Livingston is yours now! Take very good care of him!"

"I will Grammy!" Kel promised again as he gave Livingston a big squeeze!

CHAPTER FOUR
ANTICIPATION

That evening, after supper was finished and dinner dishes done, the boys thanked their grandparents for the gifts as everyone said their goodbyes and then Grammy and Papa headed home. Kel wanted nothing more than to go into his room to play with Livingston, but Momma said he had to take his bath first. Kel had never bathed so quickly! As soon as he finished, he ran to the living room where Momma was typing at the computer and Keenan was playing with his new puzzle.

"Are you done with your bath already, Kel?" Momma asked with surprise.

"Yes! Can I go play in my room with Livingston now?" He asked excitedly*.

Momma smiled and laughed, "I've never seen you so excited to play with a stuffed animal before!"

"Well, Livingston isn't just *any* stuffed animal! He's..." Kel began, but then remembered the promise he had made to Grammy, "he's special!" He simply said and smiled. Momma smiled back at him and nodded.

Kel ran to his room and quickly climbed the ladder onto his bed where he found Livingston sitting and waiting. As soon as Livingston saw Kel he bounced up in excitement, "Are we going to play? Are we going to go on an adventure? It's been such a long time since I've had a good adventure!"

Kel stared at Livingston in disbelief and wonder. Livingston continued to bounce on the bed with a huge smile! After a moment Kel laughed and said, "Silly bunny... it's too late for an adventure tonight. It's almost bedtime, but tomorrow is Saturday and Momma said we can go hiking in the woods and have a picnic! We can have an adventure there!"

"Oh, I can't wait!" Livingston exclaimed* as he fell onto the bed, grabbed his feet and began rolling around on his back. Kel couldn't help but laugh at the little fuzzy bunny.

CHAPTER FIVE
ADVENTURE DAY

The next morning Kel woke up to find Livingston sitting on his chest looking down at him with a big smile. "It's tomorrow!" he shouted as he began to jump all over the bed. "Adventure day! Adventure day!" he chanted.

Kel leaned up on his elbows and looked at the clock on his dresser. "It's only 6:30" he moaned, "you have to be quiet or you'll wake up Keenan, and if you wake up Keenan, he'll cry and wake up Momma!"

Livingston covered his mouth with his paws and crouched down on the bed giggling. "Sorry, Kelly-Belly!" He said with a smile. Kel rolled his eyes at the new nick name and laid back down. Another moment later Livingston jumped back up, "Is it time now?" he asked excitedly.

Kel sighed and laughed as he sat up in bed knowing there would be no more sleeping. "Well, let's sneak down to the kitchen and get something to eat" he said with a groggy* voice, "then we can watch cartoons until Momma and Keenan get up, OK?"

Livingston nodded excitedly in agreement. Kel slowly climbed down the ladder and reached his arms up to catch Livingston as he hopped down off the bed. He grabbed his robe from the chair at the desk and went to the closet to put on his slippers. Then, holding Livingston, he tip-toed past Momma's room, through the living room, past Keenan's room, and down the stairs into the kitchen. Kel found a box of his favorite cereal and poured it into a bowl, then added his milk. As he was about to go into the family room to sit and eat his breakfast in front of the TV, the thought occurred* to him that Livingston must be hungry too. What do stuffed bunnies eat, he wondered... stuffed carrots? He snickered to himself then looked at Livingston and asked, "Are you hungry... I mean... do you... eat?"

Livingston shook his head and said, "No, not anymore. I used to love eating clovers, though, when I lived by the farm!" he smiled and sighed. "Now that I'm a stuffed bunny I don't get hungry anymore."

Kel was very confused. "What do you mean, 'now that you're stuffed?'" he asked as he sat on the floor in front of the TV. "Weren't you always stuffed?"

"No," Livingston answered, "I used to be a real live bunny. I lived by a farm with my mama and poppa and sisters and brothers."

"There are more of you?" Kel couldn't imagine other live stuffed bunnies in the world. Before yesterday he wouldn't have imagined even one!

A sad look came across Livingston's face as he explained, "Well, there were, but now it's only me... I'm the only one that was changed like this."

Kel gazed sorrowfully* at his little friend, then carefully asked, "What happened..." then he paused, not sure he wanted to hear the answer to his question, before cautiously* continuing, " ... to the others?"

Livingston looked down at the floor as if embarrassed or uncomfortable. He then took a long breath and Kel leaned forward listening attentively*. Just when Livingston was beginning to tell the story they were both startled to a jump by Keenan's voice yelling out for Momma from upstairs. Kel sighed in frustration* knowing what was coming next.

"Kel?" Momma called, "Will you please come get your brother from his bed? I'm just stepping into the shower!"

Kel grumbled to himself and gave Livingston an apologetic* look as he yelled up the stairs, in a voice that was much louder than need be, "YES MA'AM". He stood up looking as if he were trying to make his way out of a pool of melted marshmallow. The imaginary sticky substance was seemingly still adhered* to his feet as he made a gratuitous* effort to climb the stairs.

Livingston sat next to Kel's half-eaten cereal, now all mushy in the bowl, being quite thankful for the interruption. He didn't want to tell such a sad tale now, and ruin a day potentially* filled with fun and adventure. As he sat there, still a bit melancholy*, a thought suddenly crossed his mind which instantly brought a smile and glow to his little face! *"Keenan and Momma are awake!"* he thought to himself, *"which means that it won't be long now until we go on our outing!!"* He got so excited at the idea that he could barely contain himself! He couldn't wait to get started! Oh, what adventures they would have!

CHAPTER SIX
PREPARATION*

After breakfast Momma got Keenan dressed then went down to the kitchen to make their picnic lunch. Meanwhile, upstairs in the living room, Kel rummaged through the craft drawer in the big bureau* until he found some felt, scissors, and a stapler. Livingston sat waiting, not very patiently, while Kel worked with quiet and intense* concentration. When the boy finally announced that he had finished his masterpiece Livingston sprung to his feet as if launched* from a catapult*! He couldn't wait to see what Kel had made and he silently hoped it was for him! Sure enough, it was! Kel made Livingston a little coat and a pair of boots for their hike. They weren't exactly the work of Versace* or Armani*, but they were his and he had never owned clothes before, so he was thrilled beyond measure! Kel helped him into his new outfit and looked at him appraisingly*.

"Yep! Perfect fit!" He proclaimed* with pride! Livingston nodded joyfully in agreement and began to strut as if on a catwalk* in front of a crowd of fashion aficionados*.

It wasn't long before Momma announced that it was time to get their jackets on and head to the park. Kel's eyes got wide as he realized he wasn't even dressed yet! He ran to his room and started frantically* digging through his dresser in search for something to wear. He flung t-shirts and shorts all over the room until he finally found just the right outfit. He chose a pair of cargo jeans, so his legs wouldn't get scratched up by branches or twigs and he figured all the pockets would be great for carrying everything they would need for their exploration*, a short-sleeved t-shirt, and a hoodie just in case it got cold while they were hiking. He dressed as quickly as he could then put on his hi-top tennies and laced them all the way up to help keep pebbles from getting into his shoes and bugs from biting at his ankles. He looked himself over in the mirror and was completely satisfied that he was dressed appropriately* for anything that the day may bring.

He then started to mine through his closet searching for the tools he would need. He collected a flashlight, a pocket knife, the compass Papa had given him for his birthday last year, a pad of paper and box of crayons (for doing rubbings), a small plastic container with a screen on the top that was made for collecting cool bugs, a handkerchief, a handful of army men, a disposable camera from his last school field trip that still had a few pictures left to take, and an army issue folding shovel that his Uncle Tony had given him. He placed the knife, compass and flashlight into his jeans pockets and put all the larger and less crucial* items into his backpack.

He could hear Momma in the living room now, getting Keenan into his jacket; a telltale* sign that they were about to leave. He took one last look around the then, grabbing his baseball hat from the hook on the back of his bedroom door, hurried out. He found Momma waiting for him by the front door holding a cooler in one hand and Keenan's hand in the other. He fetched Livingston from the floor by the bureau, where he had left him, then looked at Momma.

F.Thoms

"Did you pack Capri Suns?" Kel asked skeptically*.

"Of course I did!" Momma told him in a tone that suggested he was silly to think she would have forgotten.

"What about carrots?" He checked.

"Yes Sir!" Momma ensured looking at him with a slight smirk and an eyebrow raised in amusement*.

"And Cheerios to feed the squirrels?" He said crossing his arms over his chest and grinning proudly, sure he had gotten her this time.

"In the basket!" She crowed! "Now, let's get going! We're losing daylight!" She declared as she ushered* the crew out the door.

To Kel, the short one-mile drive seemed to take forever. He couldn't wait to get to the park where he could get Livingston alone again, so they could talk some more. He so badly wanted to hear the story Livingston had to tell. He couldn't imagine what in the world could have turned Livingston from a real rabbit to a stuffed bunny, and why only him... why not the rest of his family? The crunching of the gravel beneath the tires announced to him that it wouldn't be long before he would get the answers to the questions swimming in his head.

CHAPTER SEVEN
THE PICNIC

As the car came to a stop he gathered up Livingston, unbuckled his seat belt and strapped on his backpack before springing from the car like a jack-in-the-box at its melodic prime*! Momma had barely time to get Keenan unbuckled and out of his car seat when Kel asked if he could run ahead to the picnic spot. His face was lit up with such excitement that Momma didn't have the heart to say no.

The second he got the OK, he took off like a race horse out of the gate! He ran up the trail leading through a small speckling* of pine trees and lilac bushes to a clearing adorned* with picnic tables, a few small pavilions*, two drinking fountains and an area staged with enough playground equipment to accommodate* at least a couple dozen children. As he ran past, Kel tossed his backpack on the closest picnic table and darted into the maze of red wood bridges and tunnels. As soon as he found a corner where he was confident they would have some privacy, Kel sat Livingston in front of him and waited.

"I thought we would never be alone!" Livingston said with exasperation*! "I was starting to get really bored!" he complained. He then leapt to his feet with excitement and asked, "Is it time? Can we go on our adventure now?"

Kel smirked and told him, "Not yet. We have to wait for Momma and Keenan, then have lunch. After that we can go off on our own for a little bit and explore!"

Livingston sighed impatiently then plopped down on his bottom and slouched forward as if the waiting was causing him actual physical pain.

Kel looked around to ensure that there was no one nearby to overhear their conversation. He then gave Livingston an anticipatory* look and said, "Well... while we're waiting you can tell me your story to help pass the time." He smiled hopefully at the bunny.

"What story?" Livingston asked with false ignorance*.

"The story of your family and how you became a stuffed bunny!" Kel said with a smirk, aware that Livingston knew exactly what he was talking about.

"Oh... that story" the bunny said with a furrow*. "That's a boring story. We could go explore the tunnels while we wait instead." He tried his best to give a big smile, though it was difficult while remembering something so sad.

Kel's face drooped into a slight pout as he gave his little friend his best puppy dog eyes... the look he uses on Momma when he really wants to stay up a bit later on a school night. It seldom* worked with her, but he was hoping it would have more effect on Livingston.

It didn't seem to, however, as Livingston looked at Kel thoughtfully for a moment and finally said, "You don't want to hear about all that stuff now."

Kel looked at Livingston pleadingly*, "Yes I do! What happened to your family? How did you get turned into a stuffed bunny? When did it happen? How did my Grammy get you? Who..."

"OK, ok, ok..." Livingston interrupted, "if I tell you about it while we wait will you stop asking me all these questions?" He asked with exasperation. "You're making me dizzy!" He added with a slight giggle.

Kel smiled sheepishly* then nodded.

"OK, well..." Livingston began, "I don't know exactly how long ago it was, just that it seems like forever!" He settled into his seat as a thoughtful look came across his face.

After a long pause while he decided where to start, he continued, "There was a small farm surrounded by woods that were filled with lilac bushes amidst* all the trees and more clover than one bunny could eat in his whole life!!" Livingston gazed into the distance imagining the home he once loved.

Shaking his head to release himself from his daydream he went on, "I lived in a burrow* on the edge of the farm with my family. The people who ran the farm, The Miller's, were really nice... especially Emily." A sad look filled Livingston's eyes as he said her name. "Emily..." he repeated quietly. "She was my best friend. She even planted a garden just for us! It was filled with cabbage and carrots and turnips and radishes... Mmmmm!" Livingston squinched his eyes, smiled and rubbed his plush little belly. "It was like being in heaven!!"

After a moment his little smile faded to a frown. "Well, it would've been like heaven if it hadn't been for Orthon." He murmured with a scowl that appeared to be of both contempt* and fear.

Kel looked at Livingston curiously and asked, "Who's Orthon?"

"Orthon," the bunny explained, "was the biggest, ugliest, and meanest coyote I had ever seen!" Livingston shuddered and then was quiet.

Kel tried to think of what to say. He had so many questions, but he was afraid to ask. He reached out and rubbed his bunny on the head. Livingston looked up at him and smiled ever so slightly. They were both equally thankful to hear Momma's call that disrupted* the awkward* silence. Kel got up and gently picked up his bunny before heading over to the picnic table where Momma had lunch all laid out for them.

Kel took his seat at the table and placed Livingston on the bench beside him using his backpack to prop the bunny up in a seated position. While the family ate lunch Kel thought about what Livingston had told him. *He was a real rabbit once upon a time, with a real family.* The thought was so hard for the little boy to comprehend*, but then, a stuffed bunny talking and moving as if he were alive was a bit far from grasp as is, so why would the fact that he used to be an actual living bunny be any further from reality? When they had finished lunch Kel quickly helped Momma clean up then collected his bunny and his backpack and asked if he could go explore the trails a bit.

Momma looked at him with serious contemplation* on her face. "I don't know Kel." She said with a thoughtful furrow, "You are a bit young to be wandering the woods alone."

Kel looked up at Momma, "I won't go far! I'm almost 9 now! I'll stay on the trails" he pleaded and then added smugly*, "and, besides... I have a compass!" Momma folded her arms across her chest and sighed heavily. Kel knew that meant she was about to give in, so he added a final, "Pleeeeeeease?" with the sweetest face he could manage.

There it was! The smile of submission* that he had been hoping for! "Oh... alright," she started to say. Kel barely let her finish before he was off and running. "But be back in one hour! And don't leave the trails! Don't get lost!" she yelled after him and added a final, "MAKE GOOD CHOICES!" in a much louder voice, yet doubtful she was heard. She furrowed her brow unsure of her decision. *Too late now*, she thought as her oldest son disappeared into the trees.

CHAPTER EIGHT
THE ADVENTURE BEGINS

As soon as Kel rounded the corner of trees onto the trail, and Livingston knew they were finally alone, he popped his head up and gave Kel a huge grin. "Finally!" he said excitedly, "Our adventure!" He squirmed his way out of Kel's arms and hopped down to the ground to walk beside the boy. "So…" he said with an official sounding voice, "Where are we headed, Captain?"

Kel snickered and thought a moment. "Ooh! I know!" Kel said suddenly and with excitement announced, "I'll take you to Stone City!" He smiled and jumped up and down with such enthusiasm* that it made Livingston giggle with anticipation!

"What's Stone City?" He asked with wonder.

"Stone City is this really cool place Momma told me about. I've never been there, but she said it was right around here somewhere. I would assume it's a city made of stone, which should make it easy to find in the woods, don't you think?"

Livingston thought a moment and decided that made perfect sense, so he nodded in agreement and they started quickly up the trail to the top of a small hill. The trail split here into three separate branches. The one on the left followed along a wide and level path that appeared to have no turns for quite some time. The one to the right dipped down a bit, went back up a steeper hill then curved further to the right and out of view. The one in the middle was a narrow path that dipped way down to a rocky hollow, and then appeared to get even narrower before vanishing into the bushes.

They looked as far as they could in each direction then looked at each other. As if rehearsed*, they both pointed in the same direction and said, in unison*, "That one!" They had, of course, chosen the path that seemed to offer the most exciting quest*. Laughing at their unanimous* decision, they continued down the path in the middle.

Kel slipped a little as they made their way down the steep trail. After regaining his footing, he looked to see if Livingston had noticed and when he was sure he did he smiled sheepishly and advised the bunny to walk carefully with a slightly embarrassed snicker. Finally, they reached the rocky hollow, thankfully, with no further mishaps.

The path opened up here from the original 1 ½ to 2-foot width to a roundish area of about 5 foot in diameter*. Large rocks and dense* thicket pushed at the edges of what seemed like a small bowl in which they now stood. Beyond that were trees that looked very old, by size and condition, standing as if waiting for the boulders to move aside, open the gate of thicket and allow them access to the hollow. The floor of the bowl was carpeted with clover and smaller rocks of all different shape, size and color while slightly larger stones seemed to be directing them to one edge of the hollow where they found the way out down another small path.

Actually, to call it a path would be almost an exaggeration*, as it wasn't really much more than a void* in the thicket where the grass seemed to be matted down a bit by the animals that lived nearby. As a matter of fact, it slowly became so narrow that it was almost not even recognizable* as a trail at all. Just when Kel was beginning to fear they wouldn't be able to squeeze through the brush and thicket for much longer before the trail was completely inaccessible*, he noticed an opening to the right which led them to a much wider walkway making the trek* a bit more comfortable. What they gained in clearance*, however, they slowly lost in footing as the unsteady rocks and stones on the trail seemed to have quickly chased away all the soft grass, commandeering* the path for their own.

As the two explorers made their way down the gradual* decline* they were careful not to twist an ankle on the stones that now completely covered the trail. Kel couldn't help thinking about the Wizard of Oz and wondering what they would find at the end of this road. The canopy* of trees grew so thick here that they hadn't even noticed the dark and angry clouds that had slowly moved in to hide the sun. They did notice, however, the chilly breeze that danced around them now, its cold touch awakening all the goose bumps on Kel's arms. He reached into his backpack for his hoodie then quickly pulled it over his head. Only a moment later the rain started pouring down with a vengeance*!

CHAPTER NINE
THE STORM

The two young explorers, getting wetter and colder by the minute, began to move as quickly as they could manage to try to find some sort of shelter from the storm. They made it to the bottom of the rocky slope and followed the trail as it curved to the left, only to find that there was yet another hill to climb down. They were happy to see this hill was much shorter than the last, they also found it to be a bit more treacherous* of a climb as water was now flowing down the path making the rocks quite slippery. At the bottom they found themselves in a small clearing, about twice the size of the rocky hollow they had been in before. There was a tiny pool forming in the center from the downpour.

Kel looked around, desperately searching for anywhere to hide from the cold and rain and finally spotted some sort of tall structure* beyond the trees, just past the clearing. He grabbed up Livingston and ran towards it. As he approached the structure he realized it was a large stone silo. He leaned into the opening at the bottom and was disappointed to find that it had no roof.

It would definitely help guard them from the wind, but it would give no safety from the rain.

He looked around the area and noticed what appeared to be a wall about three feet tall and made of large stones mortared* into place. As they got closer, he realized that the wall continued all the way around a big square with an opening about 2 ½ feet wide between the two ends. The floor within the walls was a few feet below ground-level and was also made of stone and mortar. To one end there was a small structure that appeared to have been a fire place once upon a time which led Kel to believe that this must have been the basement of a house long ago. *But where had the rest of it gone*, he wondered to himself as they made their way down into the pit.

The fireplace was about four feet wide, three feet deep and tall enough that Kel only had to bend slightly when he was standing. It was also the only portion of the house they found that still had any overhead coverage. They made their way into the shelter just seconds before the rain began coming down so heavily that it looked like a bunch of waterfalls all around them! Kel could hardly even see beyond the walls of the basement.

He snuggled Livingston up to his neck as tight as he could when suddenly the sky was lit up by a long flash of lightning which was followed, almost immediately, by a deafening* thunderclap! It was so loud it made Kel jump back to the deepest corner of the big fireplace with fear. Livingston squirmed free of Kel's grip, crawled over his shoulder and curled up in the small space behind the boy. Kel turned around and huddled over his bunny, trying very hard not to cry. The flashes and the booms continued for what seemed to be an unbearably long time while the sheets of rain poured down relentlessly*. Even hidden in this alcove*, the two were still getting quite soaked by the rain blowing in on them.

Just when Kel thought he would burst into tears from pure terror, everything seemed to start quieting. He turned around and peered out from their makeshift* cave to see that the rain had, indeed, let up a slight bit. It was still raining at a decent rate, but now it was just coming straight down instead of every which way. The lighting was much further away also, and the thunder was nearly inaudible*. *Thank goodness!* Kel thought to himself. It wasn't until then that he realized that almost every muscle in his body was tensed up.

CHAPTER TEN
LIVINGSTON'S TALE

He scooted over and sat with his legs crisscrossed and leaned back against the middle of the rear wall of the fireplace. Livingston climbed up into his lap and they watched the rain quietly for a short time. Then Livingston noticed something shiny near the front corner of the fireplace. He hopped down and crawled over to get a closer look. He tried to pick it up, but it was wedged between a stone in the fireplace opening and a stone in the hearth*.

"What are you doing?" Kel asked his bunny as he leaned forward to try to see what had caught Livingston's eye.

"It's stuck!" Livingston groaned.

"What is?"

"I don't know..." Livingston said as he continued to grunt and grumble trying to free the little treasure. "Something shiny... but it's stuck in the rocks!" He added before he gave a final *grumph!* and plopped back down on his bottom with a scowl on his little fuzzy face.

"Let me give it a try!" offered Kel. He got down on his hands and knees and tried to see what was lodged* in the stones. It looked like a piece of jewelry of some sort. He grabbed his pocket knife and pried one of the stones loose freeing the trinket. With a smile of satisfaction, he showed Livingston a small bracelet made of a silver braided chain linked to either side of a small name plate. It was so tarnished and dirty that the writing on it was pretty much illegible*. He handed it to Livingston who peered at it quizzically* as he rubbed his little wet paw across it to clean it up the best he could.

When he could finally make out the letters on the name plate, he suddenly gasped and dropped the bracelet. Kel was very confused. He retrieved the bracelet and looked at it carefully. Engraved across the small silver plate was *Emily Rose.*

Still very confused, he asked, "Who's Emily Rose? Do you know her?"

Livingston looked up with a face so sad it almost broke Kel's heart. "I did." He murmured*. "A long time ago."

"What's wrong?" Kel asked quietly.

After a moment Livingston said in a small voice, "I know this place." He looked around at the remains of the old house. "This was home… Emily's home. This is where Emily Rose lived, and…" he took a long slow breath and continued, "this is where she died." He covered his face with his paws and drooped his ears down like a curtain in front of his face to hide himself.

Kel reached over to pet his bunny on the head. He wanted to ask so many questions, but he knew this wasn't the time. A few moments later he heard Livingston begin to speak in such a small voice that Kel was unable to make out the words at first. Livingston finally uncovered his face and began to tell his story.

"I told you about the little girl, Emily, that took care of me back when I lived on the farm as a real bunny. One day she told me that they were going to be leaving to visit family in Door County, WI for a long weekend. She was upset because she was worried about leaving us home alone for so many days. That night I saw her in her window making a wish on the night star like she always does. This time, though, she was crying. I could hear her say, "Please watch over my bunnies, especially Livingston. He is such a special friend. Please take care of him while I'm away!" It made me sad and at the same time made me feel safe because I knew that a wish from such a special little girl would surely come true. The next morning her family packed up the car and she came to say goodbye to me. She hugged me and gave me a kiss. She was crying and one of her tears fell on my ear. I will never forget it." He sat quiet for a few seconds with a melancholy* look on his little face.

The bunny cleared his throat then continued with his story. "They left the dog, Shep, tied up to keep guard over the chicken coop so Orthon wouldn't get any of the chickens. Usually Shep would keep Orthon away from us too. I was in the garden that Emily had planted for us, collecting some food to take back to our burrow. Some other rabbits from the warren* were there too. They started running off and I didn't know why. I gathered up what I could and started hurrying back towards our burrow as well when I heard Shep barking. That's when I saw Orthon run from the direction of the chicken coop. When I saw that he had spotted me I dropped all the food I was carrying and ran as fast as I could to the burrow." He furrowed his tiny brow as he explained, "I didn't even think about the fact that he would be able to follow me and find out where the warren was hidden. I led him right to it." Livingston once again began to sob.

Kel picked him up and cradled him. "I'm sure it wasn't your fault! Coyote's can almost always find rabbit hide-outs just by scent." Kel said, trying to console* his friend.

"Well," Livingston said quietly, "I don't know exactly what happened after that." He crawled down from Kel's arms and sat next to him.

"What do you mean?" Kel inquired*.

"I was running as fast as I could, but Orthon was so much faster!" He shuddered a bit as he said, "I was sure I was a goner!! Suddenly everything went dark. Next thing I knew I woke up and I was... like this." He said gesturing down to his plush little body. "Orthon had never even touched me." He shrugged and added, "I guess he wasn't interested in a stuffed bunny."

Kel tried to process what had been said, then asked, "What happened to you after that? How did my Grammy get you? What happened to Emily?"

Livingston thought for a moment and said, "I'm not completely sure what happened, to be honest. When I woke up so much time had gone by." He explained. "The warren was gone. Emily had grown up and had a family of her own. Her daughter, Emily Rose, was the one that found me out in the brush." A sweet smile brightened Livingston's face. "She took me into the house and cleaned me all up. When she showed me to her mama, the first Emily, her mama said, 'That bunny reminds me of my pet rabbit that lived here on the farm when I was a little girl. His name was Livingston.' So that's what Emily Rose named me!" He said with a huge grin.

"So, Emily Rose kept me and we were together all the time!" He continued, "She let me sleep in her bed with her and she took me with her everywhere she went! She was my best friend and I was hers!" He smiled and hugged himself.

"What happened to her?" Kel asked carefully.

Livingston's smile slowly faded. "One day, when Emily Rose was eight years old, three years after she found me, there was a horrible storm. Lightning struck a big oak tree next to the house." He peered out from the fireplace and searched for a moment. Then he pointed to a big stump just a few feet from the back of the house. "Right there." Kel looked over and saw that it looked like it had been burned at one point. Livingston sighed heavily and continued, "The tree was on fire and it fell into the house. The fire spread so quickly and there was so much smoke! Emily Rose and I were up on the top of her bunk bed and the smoke was so thick. She was crying and holding me close to her." He paused, took a slow breath, swallowed hard, and said, "The next thing I remember was being put into a box and hearing some women speaking to each other. The one lady was saying to the other, 'Poor Mr. Miller. I don't know what he is going to do now.' Then the other woman said that the room didn't even look like the fire had touched it. The first one told her that it hadn't really made it into the bedrooms, but there was just so much smoke and something about the poor little girl and her poor mother."

Kel gasped and hugged his bunny. "Oh, Livingston! I'm so sorry! That's horrible!"

Livingston nodded slightly and said, "Well, her Daddy was so upset that he couldn't even look at me. He didn't want me around anymore so he donated me, along with some of Emily Rose's other things."

"That's how Grammy got you?" Kel asked.

"Kind of," Livingston replied, "a woman bought me from a church rummage sale and she cleaned me up, mended me, and put me in her gift shop. Then one day another woman bought me for her daughter."

"The woman that bought you was my Grammy's mom?" Kel asked.

"Yes," said Livingston, "and then I lived with your grammy. It wasn't until her mama died that I was able to actually begin to talk and stuff." Livingston thought for a moment and said, "I think it was her tear that fell on my ear that did it. Like when Emily's tear fell on my ear when I was a real rabbit just before I was changed into a stuffed bunny."

"Maybe." Kel said with a shrug before noticing that the rain had finally stopped. "Look!" he exclaimed, "it's not raining anymore!"

CHAPTER ELEVEN

TIME TO HEAD HOME

Neither of them had noticed how dark it had gotten because of the storm. "How long have we been here?" Kel asked with a worried expression. "Momma's going to be so worried! We are in so much trouble! We better get back!" He jumped up and picked up Livingston before climbing out of the fireplace and up the stairs out of the house.

As they neared the silo Livingston jumped out of Kel's arms and ran over to another stone structure that was just a fraction of the size of the house foundation*. "This used to be the chicken coop!" he informed Kel excitedly. Then he ran to an area of the yard that had long been overgrown, but beneath the weeds and vines they could see a very short fence. "And this was the garden that Emily planted for us!" He said quickly then darted towards a briar patch at the base of a very large oak tree yelling, "And this is where the warren was!" He began to dig frantically.

Kel ran over to him and grabbed him up. "Livingston, we *have* to go! Momma's going to be so angry!"

Livingston sighed and nodded then asked, "Can we come back here someday?"

"Yes," Kel assured him, "and I think we should bring Grammy too! She'll want to see this!"

They started back towards the silo and down the path that led them there. When they made their way back to where they thought the clearing had been all they found was a small pond. They searched around the area for the rocky path back to the hollow, but couldn't find it. The only opening they saw was a small brook coming down a hill feeding into the pond.

Kel looked around in confusion. "Where did the trail go? Wasn't it right here somewhere?"

Livingston climbed up to Kel's shoulder to get a better view. "I don't know. Maybe this is the wrong way. Where's the clearing?"

"I don't know" replied Kel. He turned around and backtracked a short way when they found another trail that had been blocked by fallen branches. "Oh," Kel said with relief, "the storm must have knocked these down and covered the path! That's why we missed it!"

He maneuvered over the barricade and headed down the path. The two walked on for quite a while as the night grew even darker.

When nothing was looking familiar Kel began to get scared and the realization hit him that they were hopelessly lost!

Suddenly they heard something moving in the woods. Kel quickly ran over to an old log and crouched down behind it. Then Livingston saw it... a huge, ugly, grey coyote in the trees and it was watching *them!*

"It *can't* be!" Livingston whispered in shock. "How...?" he began, but his voice trailed off.

"What?" questioned Kel.

Livingston pointed to the coyote and quietly said, "Orthon!"

Kel spotted the beast and his eyes grew wide as he realized that it was looking directly at them!

CHAPTER TWELVE
THE CHASE

Kel leapt to his feet grabbing Livingston and ran into the woods as quickly as he could! He could hear the thumping of the coyote's paws behind him getting closer. He tried darting through the trees to lose it, but the sound kept getting closer by the second! Kel continued to run using every bit of strength he had, not taking time to look back. The thumping was so close that he thought he could even hear the heavy breath of the panting animal right behind him! The darkness made it almost impossible to see where he was going, then suddenly he was sliding and tumbling down a steep hill. He hardly even noticed the snapping sound followed by a sharp pain in his arm. What he did notice was that this had caused him to drop Livingston.

Finally, he came to a stop at the base of the hill and quickly looked back to see where his bunny had gone. Before he could find him, though, he saw the coyote staring down at him from the top of the crevasse*. Kel jumped up and spotted Livingston caught up in the thicket only a few feet away. He glanced back up at the coyote then took a deep breath and bolted over to his bunny. At the same moment the coyote took a great leap down the steep hillside towards the boy. Kel reached Livingston and quickly freed him from the grip of the thorns. Just as he was about to turn and run he looked up to see the vicious* animal lunging towards him. He quickly dove head first into the thicket, not knowing what else he could do. The coyote landed with a heavy thud on the ground where Kel had just been standing, then turned towards the thicket with his head lowered and his teeth bared. He stared ominously at Kel and Livingston while making the most dreadful growl from deep in his throat. Kel crouched back as far as he could manage, but the thorns were tearing into his arms through his hoodie. He was petrified* with fear! Having no other recourse*, he began to cry out as the coyote got so close that Kel could smell his wet fur and his vile* breath! He hugged Livingston as close as he could and squinched his eyes closed tight! Suddenly he was startled and confused by a loud bang that almost sounded like fireworks. He slowly opened his eyes to find the coyote lying lifeless on the ground in front of him. A second later there was a bright light shining right at him.

He looked up to see what it was, but the light was blinding. He glanced back down at the coyote, only inches away from him and his head began to spin from confusion and pure exhaustion. He barely noticed the light getting closer to him before everything went dark.

CHAPTER THIRTEEN
THE RESCUE

"Kel, can you hear me? Kel? Do you know where you are?" The child was woken by a man's voice that he didn't recognize.

"Am I in heaven?" he asked groggily.

"No, silly boy" This was a voice he *did* recognize! He opened his eyes and tried very hard to focus. Through the blur he saw her.

"Momma!" He cried and went to throw his arms around her, but she stopped him.

"Careful, now, sweetness!" she said to him softly. "Your arm is broken. You need to lie still now!" She leaned over and hugged him gently and gave him a tender kiss on the bridge of his nose, then continued, "You've had quite a night! You had me worried sick!"

When his eyes finally cleared, he looked around to find that they were in the parking lot of the park. There were flashing lights all around him and the sun was just beginning to peek out over the horizon. "What time is it?" He asked Momma.

"Almost 6:30 in the morning." She answered, "We've been searching for you for nearly 18 hours!"

"Where's Livingston?" he asked with a pang of panic.

Momma smiled and said, "He's right here, sweetness!" then she laid the stuffed bunny on Kel's chest.

Kel hugged Livingston with his good arm as some men lifted his gurney* into the back of an ambulance. Momma climbed in and sat next to him holding his hand. Just as Kel began to drift back off to sleep he heard Livingston whisper into his ear, "I can't wait for our *next* adventure!"

Kel's eyes popped wide open, "Our *NEXT* adventure??"

THE END

EPILOGUE

Kel sat in his bed reading a book he had already read three times. Livingston sat beside him playing absent-mindedly with some army men. They were both extremely bored. There was nothing to do. Kel's left arm was still in a cast, and since he was left handed he couldn't even draw. He was forbidden to go outside to play so they had been cooped up in the house for nearly two weeks already. The only time they got to go outside, other than to go to school, was when they were with Momma and then she would never let Kel out of her sight or let him do anything fun for fear of him hurting his arm. He still had another month in the cast and couldn't wait for it to be off!

"What do you want to do?" whined Livingston, "I'm soooo bored!"

"I don't know," answered Kel, "we could play cards I guess."

"We played cards all day yesterday!" Livingston complained. "We need an adventure!" he said with a mischievous* smile.

Kel smirked and said, "Yeah, well, our last adventure got us in enough trouble to last us for a while! There is no way Momma's going to let us go that far alone again!" He frowned at the bunny and sighed heavily.

"Well," Livingston offered, "we don't have to go off into the woods this time. We can do something else... go somewhere else!"

"Like where?" Kel asked skeptically.

Livingston smiled at the boy and said, "Oh... I don't know. How about... the moon?!"

GLOSSARY

accumulate: to pile up, collect, or gather. To grow in amount or mass.

accommodate: to have room for

adhered: *to stick or cling firmly*

adolescence: the period in a person's life between childhood and adulthood.

adorned: to add beauty to; decorate.

aficionados: an enthusiast or fan, as of an art, a sport, or a pastime.

alcove: a partly enclosed area of a room.

amidst: in the middle of; among; amid.

amusement: something that amuses or entertains; fun.

anticipation: the act or process of anticipating; the condition of expecting or hoping.

anticipatory: of, feeling, or expressing anticipation.

apologetic: expressing or wanting to express regret, as for an error or an offense.

appraisingly: (the adverb derivative of appraise) to judge the quality or nature of.

appropriately: (the adverb derivative of appropriate) right for the purpose; proper.

Armani: Giorgio Armani. born 1936, Italian fashion designer, noted for his restrained classical style

attentively: (the adverb derivative of attentive) paying close attention.

awkward: embarrassed or embarrassing; uneasy

burrow: a hole or tunnel dug by small animals such as rabbits or moles for use as a hiding place or home.

bureau: a chest of drawers.

canopy: The uppermost layer in a forest, formed by the crowns of the trees.

catapult: an ancient weapon used to throw objects, such as large stones or arrows, at an enemy; pushed or thrown with force; thrust by or as though by a catapult.

catwalk: a narrow ramp extending from the stage into the audience in a theatre, nightclub, etc., especially as used by models in a fashion show.

cautiously: (the adverb derivative of cautious) taking care to avoid danger or trouble; careful.

clearance: the space between things that keeps them from striking against each other.

commandeering: to take by force or without authorization.

comprehend: to understand or grasp the meaning of.

confusion: the act of confusing or state of being confused.

consider: to think carefully about; reflect on.

console: to give comfort in time of loss or suffering; make less sad.

contemplation: thoughtful reflection or examination; act of contemplating.

contempt: the feeling or expression of angry disgust at something wicked, mean, or not worthy.

crevasse: a deep cleft or crack, esp. in a glacier or in the earth's surface.

crucial: very important; deciding the success or failure of something.

deafening: to overcome with loud noise.

decline: to slope or slant downward.

dense: having parts very close together with little space between; thick and hard to see through or penetrate.

diameter: the width of a circle, sphere, or cylinder.

disappointment: the act of disappointing; the fact or feeling of being disappointed.

disrupted: to interrupt or break off.

enthusiasm: something that causes such great interest in an activity.

exaggeration: the act or an instance of exaggerating; overstatement; to present as larger, more important, or more valuable.

exasperation: an act of exasperating or the state of being exasperated; to bother or annoy to the point of causing anger.

excitedly (the adverb derivative of excited) aroused to a condition of excitement; thrilled.

exclaimed: to speak suddenly and/or loudly and with strong feeling.

exploration: the act of investigating or examining; exploring new or unknown places.

foundation: the stone or concrete structure that holds up a building from beneath.

frantically: (the adverb derivative of frantic) very excited by worry or fear; frenzied.

frustration: a condition or instance of being frustrated; to disappoint or puzzle.

furrow: a narrow groove made in a surface, such as ones forehead from pulling the eyebrows together in worry, concern, or concentration.

gestured: a movement of one's body or face that shows feeling or thought.

gingerly: in a careful or cautious manner; warily; demonstrating care or caution.

gracious: likely to do what is polite, kind, or right.

gradual: happening by degrees that are small and even.

gratuitous: given or done without sufficient reason or justification; unwarranted.

groggy: confused, dizzy, or sleepy.

gurney: a padded hospital stretcher on wheels, used to transport patients.

hearth: the floor of a fireplace, or the stone or brick area in front of it.

ignorance: lack of education or information.

illegible: difficult or impossible to read.

inaccessible: hard or impossible to reach, approach, or attain.

inaudible: impossible to hear.

inquired: to ask to find out or learn.

intense: strong or very deep.

launched: to put in motion with force.

lodged: to be or become caught or stuck in a certain position.

makeshift: made to meet a need; not meant to last.

melancholy: suffering from or likely to suffer from sadness or depression.

melodic prime: A state or time of greatest strength or vigor of a melody.

mischievous: teasing or sly.

mortared: bricks or stones held in place by a material made from lime, sand, and water.

murmured: to make a soft, muffled, continuous sound.

nervously: acting in a fearful or anxious manner in a specific situation.

nostalgia: a longing for the past.

occurred: to appear in one's thoughts

ominous: giving a sign of future evil or trouble.

pavilions: a light building with open sides used for shelter or recreation.

petrified: Make (someone) so frightened that they are unable to move or think.

pleadingly: (adverb derivative of the word plead) to ask in a sincere or serious way.

potentially: with a possibility of becoming actual.

preparation: the act of getting something ready.

proclaimed: to say or state for the public to know.

protest: an objection or complaint.

quest: a search or pursuit.

quizzically: expressing doubt, confusion, or questioning; puzzled.

recognizable: that is or can be recognized (recognize: to identify from an earlier experience.)

recourse: the act, or an instance or process, of seeking or applying for help and/or protection.

rehearsed: to practice for a show, play, concert, or other performance.

relentlessly: without stopping or slackening; persistent or unremitting.

seldom: not often; rarely.

sheepishly: (the adverb derivative of the word sheepish) showing embarrassment, as from becoming aware of having done something foolish or stupid.

shooed: to urge (a person or animal) to leave.

skeptical: having or showing doubt; questioning.

skeptically: in a skeptical manner.

smugly: confident of or satisfied with oneself to the point of annoying other people; complacent.

sorrowfully: (the adverb derivative of the word sorrowful) characterized by or expressing sorrow; mournful.

speckling: a pattern or expanse of sparse dots.

steep: having a sharp slope or slant.

structure: anything that has been built.

submission: the act or an instance of submitting. (submit: to give in to the will or power of another.)

suspicious: without trust.

tedious: long and boring; dull; wearisome.

telltale: any of various devices or objects that serve to indicate desired information.

treacherous: full of danger or risk.

trek: a slow or difficult trip.

unanimous: in complete agreement.

unison: speaking all at the same time.

ushered: to lead, escort, or show.

vengeance: (with a vengeance) with great force or fury; violently; to an extreme, excessive, or surprising degree.

Versace: Donatella Versace, born 1955, Italian fashion designer and businesswoman; creative director of the Versace group from 1997. Also, her brother, Gianni 1946-97, Italian fashion designer.

vicious: wicked; evil; likely to be cruel or violent; fierce.

vile: extremely bad, disgusting, or unpleasant.

void: an empty space.

warren: a network of many rabbit burrows.

ACKNOWLEDGMENTS

I would like to give my most heartfelt thanks to Florence Thoms, who, at the age of 102 years old, did several of the illustrations in this book. She is a marvel and such a wonderfully remarkable woman! She is my hero!

Printed in the United States
By Bookmasters